CONFESSIONS of an
Ageing Football
Player

NICK OWEN
Illustrated by PAUL WARREN

AuthorHouse™ UK
1663 Liberty Drive
Bloomington, IN 47403 USA
www.authorhouse.co.uk
UK TFN: 0800 0148641 (Toll Free inside the UK)
UK Local: 02036 956322 (+44 20 3695 6322 from outside the UK)

Because of the dynamic nature of the Internet, any web addresses or links contained in this book may have changed
since publication and may no longer be valid. The views expressed in this work are solely those of the author and do not
necessarily reflect the views of the publisher, and the publisher hereby disclaims any responsibility for them.

Any people depicted in stock imagery provided by Getty Images are models,
and such images are being used for illustrative purposes only.
Certain stock imagery © Getty Images.

This book is printed on acid-free paper.

ISBN: 979-8-8230-8454-3 (sc)
ISBN: 979-8-8230-8453-6 (e)

Print information available on the last page.

Published by AuthorHouse 10/10/2023

authorHOUSE®

The Group Stage

Match 1.   Brazil 2014–2015 My Team.

The final score—73–nil! Those were the days—moments of glory on the school playing field on a foggy Wednesday afternoon. When the final whistle went, your schoolmates would gather around you, beaming their small faces at you from every conceivable direction as they congratulated you fulsomely on the twenty-three hat-tricks you just completed in your team's undeniable slaughter of the opposition.

The juniors from Mrs Myrtle's class were never going to stand up to the superior firepower of Mr Thompson's fourth years, and your part in their downfall was heralded as the natural climax of a long and muddy school football season.

In those days, England won the World Cup for the first (and only?) time, and the nation *rejoiced, rejoiced, rejoiced*. In the course of that fateful autumn season when I moved primary schools seven times, I was able to become Roger Hunt, Nobby Stiles, Bobby Moore, Martin Peters, George Cohen, Georgie Best, and Jimmy Greaves in three short months. I was playing footie with mates in a school classroom, at the park, in the garage, in a potato field, down an anonymous dirt track, in the kitchen, and even once on a proper football field. We all became our own heroes overnight and never looked back, plotting our own ways to football fame and fortune ever since.

We all, of course, went our different ways: Roger disappeared into medical supplies, Georgie into pub management, and Jeff into the funeral business. But me, I stayed lean and mean, waiting for the next major football opportunity. World Cups have come and gone, but I feel it in my bones. Brazil 2014 may just be the one where I make my mark and relive the joy of twenty-three hat-tricks against the juniors.

Neymar, Messi, Oxlade-Chamberlain—you have all been warned. This year is my year.

Match 2.　Chile 3–0 Australia (I will be that carioca!)

You're not going to believe this, but it's true (enough). Me and the lads are out on the park tonight, cheering and jeering each other as is usual for us on a Thursday night, when, what do you know, a postman rides up to us on his pre–Second World War rickety-rackety bike, rummages around in his sack, and extracts what looks like a flea-bitten telegram. He looks around at us all and our collection of muddy knees, torn shirts, and scuffed boots. Eventually, his quizzical gaze focuses on me.

"It's for you?" He's adopted that annoying upturn of vocal intonation so beloved of soap stars from the Antipodes. I nod and reach out for his missive. I rapidly tear it open, wanting to get on with our park kickabout, but upon reading its contents, I slump to the ground in disbelief.

"You OK?" asks the postie.

I nod, partially dazed and completely confused. It has transpired that in the build-up to this year's World Cup, our national football team has had to remove several lower-ranked footballers from its squad due to some mysterious case of food poisoning that they picked up from some mysterious source. The management has been forced, right at the last minute, to survey the stats of some of our nation's more modest talent from the league tables that yours truly diligently fills in every week in my capacity as team secretary. And they have concluded that the best player in our league—as defined by goals, assists, back passes, and good intentions—is yours truly. I have consequently been called up to join the national squad to play for our beloved country in what is, let's face it, the pinnacle of all sporting achievement. Ever.

There's little time to hang around. My flight tickets are waiting for me at the airport. My bags have been packed by the team's coach, who has had to spend yet more time in the poisoned atmosphere that is the modern jetliner fuselage to collect me and my old socks. And my diet from now on will be severely restricted to no fewer than 15,000 calories a day. It's going to be difficult to be jettisoned into the stellar attention of international football stardom, but I'm as ready for it as I always have been.

I have waited all my life for this moment. It won't hurt my team to wait that little bit longer for me to arrive and collect what is rightfully mine—the lifting of the Jules Verne trophy on Saturday, 13 July, in Rio de Janeiro. First stop, though—Bogotá—and an old jeweller I need to settle some scores with.

Match 3.   Colombia 3–0 Greece (Settling old football scores is easy.)

It occurs to me as the plane drops steeply through the Andes towards Bogotá that life is not what it seems. One day, you're a hick from the sticks punting an old piece of leather from pillar to post with your schoolmates, workmates, or enemy soldiers, and the next, you're slipping through the egg timer of life. You find yourself with the elite of the elite, hobnobbing with the glitterati, chatterati, and flitterati as you wander aimlessly through the duty-free shop looking for the biggest bar of Toblerone you can fit in your trouser pocket without being mistaken for a suicide bomber with a nasty surprise in his trousers.

You would be amazed at who loiters in duty-free these days. Usually, I rush through in a panic, looking for the rapidly disappearing Ryanair flight to Belfast. But today, with nothing to do but wait six hours for the next connection to the deepest Amazonian jungle, I am able to saunter through duty-free like I haven't a care in the world, my carioca trilby perched jauntily atop my head and my trusty footie boots hung around my neck. There can be no mistaking where I'm going—to join my team as an emergency stand-in player for our indisputable forthcoming World Cup triumph.

Today, I am inwardly startled by and externally nonchalant about the stellar members of the football universe who also have been waylaid from reaching Brazil's welcoming football beaches and who are, like me, trolling through duty-free. There's Alex Gerrard deep in conversation with Elke Pfingstein (one-time amour of Franzie Beckenbauer, to the uninitiated amongst you). Elke looks a million dollars, which is unsurprising given the hip replacement surgery she's had over the last forty-nine years. And oooohh, look over there! What's *he* doing here at this time of this week, of all weeks! He should be in São Paulo hanging out with his FIFA mates, not lurking around the duty-free in Bogotá airport! Can't wait to tell the mates back home about this little sighting!

But I can't malinger any longer; my flight is called, my business in Bogotá done, and I am off to join my fellow teammates, who no doubt will be as delighted to see me as I am delighted to see them.

Match 4.   Italy 0–1 Little Chalfont (Into the heart of darkness)

When I was ten, I scored my first goal ever in a school football match. I was standing somewhere on the pitch, facing in the right kind of direction and peering into the mist, which hovered over the mud. And slowly, out of the kingfisher blue of the sky looped this large leather ball towards me. I could see the panel stitching as if I were looking at it through a microscope—not the usual telescope I needed when it came to trying to navigate my way around the football pitch of life.

I stepped slowly towards the ball, slowly stuck out my foot, and saw the ball ricochet off it slowly and sail even more slowly from whence it came, through the space defined by the silhouetted goalposts, and into the flaming autumnal sunset. I scored a goal, I found out later, by a "half volley".

All hell broke loose. I screamed, turned, and ran down the opposite end of the pitch, my arms flailing in every direction. My teammates chased after me, screaming. The opposition looked on, aghast at the unlikely spectacle of the boy who normally spent most of his football life engraving his name in the muddy pitch with his outsize boots celebrating scoring a goal. The whistle between the referee's lips dropped into the mud. Even the sound of Amazonian drums could be heard in the distance, battling through the inertia of suburbia.

This was unbelievable, incredible, and completely implausible as far as they all were concerned. The opposition's captain, Johnson, showed then how to react the next time I got close to kicking the ball. "Get him, he's dangerous!" he yelled. And they swooped down at me, ruthlessly depriving me of my next moment of glory by decking me, stealing the ball, and running down the other end of the pitch in a frenzied horde to hammer the point home that they were the far superior side by scoring ten easy goals in the final five minutes of the game. We lost 15–1 that afternoon. And I knew how those guys felt when they were trounced by their opposition last night.

That moment taught me all I needed to know about my future footballing destiny. I would be a permanent surprise to the opposition. They would constantly underestimate me. I would strike at the least likely moment in a manner which would leave everyone rooted to the ground, mouths fixed open in scarecrow gasps. I would be the gorilla in their midst.

In my footballing future, I would play the outcast rooted to the penalty area at the wrong end of the pitch, but my unerring sense of time, place, luck, and boredom would inevitably find me in goal-scoring chances, which I would take with alacrity.

My consequent footballing journey might have looked like it would involve a lot of lounging around in the lower divisions with nothing more to look forward to than an away fixture in Little Chalfont. But I always knew that one day, an opportunity would come sailing through that kingfisher-blue sky, begging me to grasp it, shake it, kick it, or possess it in whatever form I saw fit. I would just have to make sure I left the opposition reeling in disbelief.

So, as I step off the plane in Cayenne, French Guiana, I know that the 2014 World Cup is the fulfilment of that call of destiny. The fact that I have yet to arrive in the country to which destiny is calling me is a minor issue. I have to visit an old footballing shaman by the name of Terry Venables, who established a commune deep in the heart of the Amazon. I know that now is the time to sit at his feet, soak up his wisdom, and prepare myself for what is ahead in the coming days.

Match 5.   Brazil 1–2 Norway (The inside track on the rank outsider)

To be fit is human; to be a footballer at the 2014 World Cup divine. There's no getting away from it: being young, free, and single with the ability to wander unhindered the boulevards of Rio de Janeiro, wearing nothing but your finest-quality pink football boots, is something close to living the dream.

The good thing about being late called-up players to our national squad is that we have plenty of free time on our hands. Sure, the management do their best to suggest that we might like to attend all the matches our team is playing in, but we know that with a little nudge and a wink to Herr Capitano (as we jokingly refer to our team's coach and mentor), it's possible for us to take our foot off the pedal and while away the hours down on Copacabanana Beach.

All of you out there slogging through your daily grind in civvy street reckon that the life of an overpaid footballer is one of intense physical workouts, a mean and lean diet, and several days spent recuperating in spa baths and nuclear magnetic resonators with electrodes strapped to one's testicles. Far from it. Now that I've got an insider's view, I know the life of a latter-day gladiator is much more relaxed than anyone would believe.

The toughest part is coping with those teams for whom participation in the competition has come to an abrupt, untimely end. The Spanish and English boys have been moping around the hotel lobbies like lost mongrels over the last few hours, now that their aspirations have been crushed. The English captain (Stevie G, as they call him) and his Spanish equivalent, Cervantes, have shown some degree of self-respect when it comes to fielding questions from the nosy, noisy press. But their compadres Joe Hart and Joaquin Rodrigo have shown some pretty disgraceful behaviour. Toys and prams don't even come close to sufficing.

So, whilst those two teams pack their bags and head back to London Airport (Luton branch) and Aeropuerto de las Vacas in Torremolinos, we have been called in for a little light stretching, deep breathing, and video entertainment for the rest of the weekend. Next week will be tough, but not as tough as taking an early bath of an exit in what is proving to be, for me, the highlight of my slow-burning football career.

Match 6.   Argentina 1–2 Millwall (The return of the football flâneur)

I have wandered through the streets of Rio de Janeiro, encountered the thronged city of São Paulo, mingled with the crowds of Manaus, and allowed myself to be woven into the rich tapestry of urban Brazilian life, acknowledging no obstacle or hindrance for myself or for anyone else—all in the name of the mass spectacle that is the World Cup of 2014.

As a true flâneur—reluctant to raise a hand against anyone, especially those intimidating members of the opposite team—I have found myself in profound opposition to all who would impose their own tribal barbarism onto the world, whether in the form of local gangs, sectarian enclaves, or any other kind of baboonery. The problem is that contemporary global football depends on the activities of gangs, enclaves, and other baboons, so the lot of the flâneur, last-minute substitute players is not an easy one.

Every day, we are faced with almost insurmountable dilemmas: *Should I raise the world's awareness of the plight of the dispossessed Brazilian? Or should I just shut up for a bit longer? Should I train or should I stay in and muse on the demands the training schedule is placing on groins, knees, and Achilles tendons? Should I play or should I go?*

Fellow footballing flâneurs will appreciate the stress that is heaped upon me on an almost daily basis, but are unlikely to offer any solution of any merit. No, the fact is that the time is fast approaching when my values and aspirations will be severely tested.

The coaches are muttering about resting several of our team for later rounds of the competition, and this can only mean one thing: yours truly will get his first run out on the hallowed pitch of a World Cup stadium. Heaven help us. And me too for that matter. Words will need to be had.

Match 7.   Uruguay 2–1 England (Do I have to?)

It is of course a great honour to be picked for one's national football team. But there are times at the World Cup when even the most galactic of galacticos have to hold up their hands, look across the squad, and admit there are stronger players in front of them right here, right now, and that if they're to secure their chances of progressing to the next round, it would be wiser to choose someone else—anyone else—than yours truly.

I am not one to show false modesty and downplay my superior football talents, let me hasten to add. I am here with the best of them solely on merit, nothing to do with any ratings shenanigans that some players are muttering about. Neither do I lack the desire to play for my team, my country, my flag; on the contrary, I have been desirous in the extreme to show up willingly and turn up when needed, on time, and on budget, sporting all the regulation sportswear.

But sat here on Copacabanana Beach, idling away the hours with Sergio Mendez on the iPod and a selection of rather intriguing coconut cocktails in front of me, not to mention the sights and sounds of the locals at play, I have reluctantly realised that I am not at the top of the manager's plans when it comes to choosing the next squad who will be charged with our team's progress on this most auspicious of footballing occasions.

The pain is tangible, but I will hold myself together in as dignified a manner as possible. I will spurn any interest by the world's media and, if asked for a quote, will offer them the party line: "I'm right behind our manager." I will sacrifice my own ambition for the greater good and step back to allow younger, more talented, and better-looking players than I to step into the limelight and do what is required.

It will be tough watching the team perform from the frustratingly distant first-class hotel right next to the beach that we're having to endure, but someone has to do it. My time will come at the right time; but right now, it's time for a quick sundowner and a stroll along the promenade to contemplate the harsh reality facing the late call-up substitute footballer.

Match 8.   Mrs Myrtle's Class 5–0 Mr Thompson's Class
(Giving it back to the community, big style)

One of the great World Cup traditions, which is being honoured to the hilt in Brazil, is when teams from the world's footballing elite visit the poor children of the ghettos and spread peace and goodwill amongst the masses in the shape of new footballing skills, boxed sets of TV blockbusters, and authentically signed copies of our imminent autobiographies.

In some unfortunate cases, this is not all we leave behind. Seven shades of STDs are known to have been left behind in remote villages of the Western Cape four years ago, but decorum and the threat of legal action mean that one must draw a discreet veil over those proceedings and move on, swiftly.

At the 2014 World Cup in Brazil, however, there is no such danger of an unfortunate legacy. Our team management has elected to send myself and several other top-notch squad members into the heart of the 'burbs to share our prowess, knowledge, and empathy for mankind in the only way we know how.

I demonstrate to the admiring youth the technique of keepy-uppy and manage to keep the ball in the air using just my head for at least twenty seconds. The youth are clearly impressed. I resort to film star impressions: Russell Crowe's *Gladiator*, Sean Connery's James Bond (*Goldfinger* era), Arnold Schwarzenegger's *Terminator* (*2*, not *1*), and my pièce de résistance, the classic British classical actor Mr Bean. All have the impoverished youth of the city baying for more.

Before too long, international relations are cemented with me teaching the youth pretty much everything I know. How to make a three-egg omelette on the bonnet of a taxi, how to use an iPhone 5, and seven useful things to say if you ever visit my country and need to visit the vet are all lapped up by the locals.

This excellent example of how to spread the good news about the World Cup to all and sundry leaves everyone feeling warm and cosy: the children get to touch an iPhone, the local taxi drivers get tipped, and we international football stars feel that we have both given something to and gotten something back from the local communities. Whether that something turns into a nasty viral infection is something we let the team doctor worry about as he stocks us up with top-grade penicillin on the coach back to our luxury hotel.

For the time being, all is well in our big, happy, global world of football. And we all carry a warm, rosy glow with us back to the bar, where we sip cocktails till dawn and reflect soberly on the state of humanity and what differentiates us—intergalactic football stars—from the impoverished and unfortunate youth of the 'burbs.

Match 9.   Iran 1–2 Saudi Arabia (Chickens and lions coming home to roost)

We're at the end of the first phase of the Brazilian World Cup, and it's sad to see so many familiar faces look like they've just died and gone straight to the hell of their domestic leagues whilst the more talented ones amongst us have secured our victories and gotten ourselves into the "round of the last sixteen", as it's biblically referred to.

The Lampards, Aboubakars, and Cucurachas of the world will soon be sullenly climbing those aeroplane steps, casting long, lingering, envious glances at us—the galacticos who have fought like tigers, struggled with demons, and tussled with incalcitrant barmaids in our quest for footballing superiority.

And all I can say in sympathy is a phrase which has stayed with me since my earliest football days, a phrase which has been a lesson in life that I have treasured, a phrase which has haunted me since the age of six, when a much older player by the name of Pele ridiculed me in the schoolyard after biting me on the backs of my knees with his long Dracula fangs:

"LOS-ER! LOS-ER! LOS-ER!"

It was one of those extremely beneficial life experiences which made me what I am. After that day in the schoolyard with Pele, I vowed to exact my revenge on the players who thought they were cool but, in fact, were dreary; the players who thought they were athletes but, in fact, were big, fat, chinless blobs; the players who thought they could turn the girls' heads with their gleaming smiles, slicked black hair, and polished canines but, in fact, could no more turn their aunties into sleeping beauties waiting for their absent princes for forever and a day because they were so damn ugly and permanently asleep.

So, Señor Lampard, Herr Aboubakar, and Mr Cucuracha, I jerk my right hand in your general direction as you board that plane with your football socks around your neck and screech at the top of my voice:

"LOS-ER! LOS-ER! LOS-ER!"

You may not notice, you may not listen, you may not even care, but you, sirs, are going home to pluck your feathers whilst I am here preening mine in the finest of footballing company. I may be a bit player, a journeyman, a team player, but there's only one thing that matters right now: I am here and you are gone.

Match 10.   England 4–2 France (Four Eyes one, Two Eyes nil)

It's come to my attention that I have been called up for a training session later this evening. One of my so-called teammates came charging up to me at lunch, where I was doing my utmost to hit my target 15,000 calories a day, and trumpeted out loud and proud for everyone to hear:

"Hey! Guess who's in the squad! It's Speccy Four Eyes!"

At which point, of course, everyone—even the most aloof of intergalactic intergalacticos—put down their forks and spoons and turned to stare at me in disbelief. I could see the thought bubbles rising out of their heads and drifting up to the restaurant ceiling, where they gently came to rest in a gentle, bobbing mass of red, white, blue, green, purple, and yellow (our away strip is something of a visual dog's dinner and gives rise to all kinds of terrible promotional aesthetics).

"Him?"

"Training?"

"Speccy Four Eyes?"

"You're 'aving a laff!'

"I'm gonna have words!"

"We're doomed!"

"I'm complaining to FIFA!"

"I'm going on strike!"

"I'm gonna bite him."

The thought bubbles blossomed into balloons, filled with the helium of indignation and disgust. "Speccy Four Eyes", as I am quaintly referred to, is clearly a source of some disgust and irritation to many within the assembled horde.

SFE is one of those phrases that other kids at school would lob about with gay abandon when we were younger. It wasn't funny then, and it's not much funnier now that I'm *ahem, ahem* years older. It was a boring insult then, and it's even more turgid now, blindingly obvious and a tedious excuse to insult me and my footballing prowess. It comes about, of course, because of my medical need to wear glasses when I'm on the football field;

without them, I'm as blind as a vampire footballer, and I can't wear contact lenses due to some mysterious hereditary condition. So, glasses it is, and glasses it will remain for as long as I can don an outsize pair of pink football boots.

The bigger concern, though, is the implication—dare I say instruction—that I shall have to don the aforesaid football boots, venture out onto the playing field at some point in the next twenty-four hours, and put my life and limbs on the line in a training session.

Don't get me wrong—I fully appreciate the need for some people to train and rehearse. But for me, the mantra "practice makes perfect" has mutated into "practice makes permanent", meaning that if I make any mistakes, they will only be entrenched with the rigours of a training schedule. I am a performance person, someone who can instantly rise to the call of the performance moment but prefers not to spend dreary hours doing drills, reciting the national anthem, and pretending to be friendly in the compulsory group hug that precedes every training session. The team will get a lot more out of me if we dispense with the sham that is the training field and just plug me into the game at the right moment.

With that thought in mind, I swallowed the last of the 15,000-calorie donut diet and hotfooted it (or rather, lounged over in a semi-casual, flâneur type of way) to the senior management team, who were locked in their bunker, planning for world domination.

"Speccy Four Eyes" I may be, but I'm blessed with a bigger vision. Expecting me to train with and endure the taunts of the wombats who make up the rest of the team is something I can see coming light years away, and not something I intend to endure any day soon.

Match 11.   England 0–1 USA (Everyone "loves" a winner)

Despite my protestations to the senior management cabal, it befell me to attend a training session late into the night, during which I was duly kicked from pillar to post and back again several times. After that, I had to succumb to the indignity of *hose-piping*: our national team's time-honoured tradition wherein the most successful players of the evening are duly accorded their rightful place in the hierarchy by the rest of the squad through a process which involves hose-pipes.

I shall not elaborate other than to say that hose-piping is one of those traditions much beloved by sophomores in American universities, geared towards bonding strangers together in mutual hatred of their community. Allegedly, it leads to greater academic performance and superior athletic achievement, and helps instil a sense of empire across the rest of the world.

For me, however, it led to no such achievement other than the pent-up wrath of decades finding vent in a nearby fast-food joint, where I managed to reach my target 15,000-calorie intake at least five times over by the end of the night. I can at least take it easy on the hot dogs for the next couple of days whilst I watch our team progress through the next phase: the biblically inspired group of sixteen.

One of the important lessons in this footballing life is that you must always look for a silver lining, no matter how cataclysmically thunderous the weather. The good thing about the training session is that I did at least manage to score the winning goal in a 1–0 victory.

It was late in the game, and I had wandered down the end of the pitch, thinking the referee had blown his whistle and was looking to get off sharpish, without having to endure the indignities of the group shower. Then all of a sudden, the ball landed at my feet and stopped. Somewhere deep in the Amazonian earth, a small vole must have moved in its sleep because the subsequent soil movement meant that the ball was raised slightly on a small vole mound. All around me, the world went dark, and the sun shone on the ball. I looked at it and then the goalposts ahead of me, and then stuck out my right foot in a tentative, proddy sort of way.

Before I could say, "Julio Inglesias", the ball shot off my foot and into the top left-hand corner of the goal. Our team was delirious. The opponents complained viciously to the referee about how I must have bitten the goalkeeper, but their protests were ignored, and the goal was allowed to stand.

Before I knew it, the final whistle had been blown, and my colleagues promptly hoisted me high into the air on their shoulders. Or rather, they tried hoisting me high into the air on their shoulders, but my 15,000-calorie intake got the better of them. They agreed to lift my right leg instead, offered thanks to the football gods for its innate skill and footballing intelligence, and then unceremoniously dumped me on the ground. At that point, they engaged in the sophomoric tradition of hose-piping, which I shall say nothing about. At least I managed to avoid the showers.

The better news is that my inspirational, intuitive skills on the pitch mean that I have been elevated up the team sheet and I now risk sitting on the bench for our game in the next phase: the canonical group of eight. I'm thinking that if this is what constitutes success, then the sooner I experience defeat, the better. Being hose-piped for winning a training session is one thing; what would happen if I unwittingly scored the winning goal in our next game doesn't bear thinking about.

Match 12.   Uruguay 1–2 Italy (Luis Suarez, the axolotls, and me)

Luis and I have been firm friends for as long as we can remember, sharing comic books, bicycles, and model aeroplanes built from balsawood kits. He came round a couple of days ago wanting to build a Messerschmitt, so we whiled away a few hours getting glue on our fingers and perpetually losing the pilot.

"Airfix kits aren't what they used to be," he mused, and I concurred. "They used to be much more fiddly; now it looks like they're built for idiots to assemble."

"It's part of our general culture of dumbing down," I replied, and he nodded thoughtfully.

"Look at these roundels, for example." He held up the little circular stickers that were meant to adorn the fuselage. "Once, you has to float them in agua to release them. Now, you has only to peel them back. Where is the skill in that? The challenge even? I disappointed." I had to agree with him. Once a thing of delicacy, the Airfix Messerschmitt roundel has now become just another piece of sticky-back plastic.

He looked dejected, so I suggested we forget Airfix for a while and check out the axolotls. They'd not seen him since the start of the World Cup and seemed to be pining for him. He brightened up at this idea, and we both made our way to the axolotl tank in the hotel bar.

Imagine our consternation when we got to the tank only to find that both axolotls had metamorphosed into tiger salamanders! Beautiful creatures they may be, but the whole point of the axolotl is that it doesn't metamorphose; its beauty is in its ugliness and all the attendant transformational potential that goes with it. The salamander is fine, but its precursor, the axolotl, is a thing of latent beauty, not manifest obviousness.

Luis was beside himself and, I have to say, didn't handle himself well. He was distraught and charged around the hotel lobby, paranoid that someone had put iodine in the axolotls' diet to accelerate their change. He was convinced—and so was I—that this was the act of a brutal, evil animal who had to be stopped at all costs from wreaking havoc on other unfinished amphibian forms.

There was no stopping him as he accused everyone he confronted, from departing football players, heading back to the ignominy of the lower reaches of Second Division football in the Urals, to managers, pundits, WAGs, FIFA officials and their WAGs, coaches, psychiatrists who were looking for jobs, medics, fans, amphibian specialists, agents, dentists, film stars, politicians, mafia bosses, and all manner of cosmetic surgeons. Even Eric Cantona received Luis's face-to-face treatment, and he hasn't quite looked the same since.

There's been enough said about Luis's recent foray into the jungle that is the Brazil World Cup, so I'm not going to say anything that will add to the myths that are being stapled to the man on a minute-by-minute basis. But if you really want to know the reason why Luis is in the state he is, just find whoever it was who converted the axolotls into salamanders, and give both of us their head on a plate.

Luis is basically a good lad, and like him, I am seething at what has happened to our amphibians. Whoever you are out there, be warned: Luis and I are after you.

Giorgio Chiellini, we're looking at you, mate.

The Group Stage Results

Match 1.   **Brazil 2014–2015 Little Chalfont**
Match 2.   **Chile 3–0 Australia**
Match 3.   **Colombia 3–0 Greece**
Match 4.   **Italy 0–1 Little Chalfont**
Match 5.   **Brazil 1–2 Norway**
Match 6.   **Argentina 1–2 Millwall**
Match 7.   **Uruguay 2–1 England**
Match 8.   **Mrs Myrtle's Class 5–0 Mr Thompson's Class**
Match 9.   **Iran 1–2 Saudi Arabia**
Match 10.   **England 4–2 France**
Match 11.   **England 0–1 USA**
Match 12.   **Uruguay 1–2 Italy**

The remaining Group A matches between Little Chalfont and the Netherlands, Brazil and Germany, and Mexico and Germany were all cancelled following a temper tantrum by Luis Suarez of Uruguay.

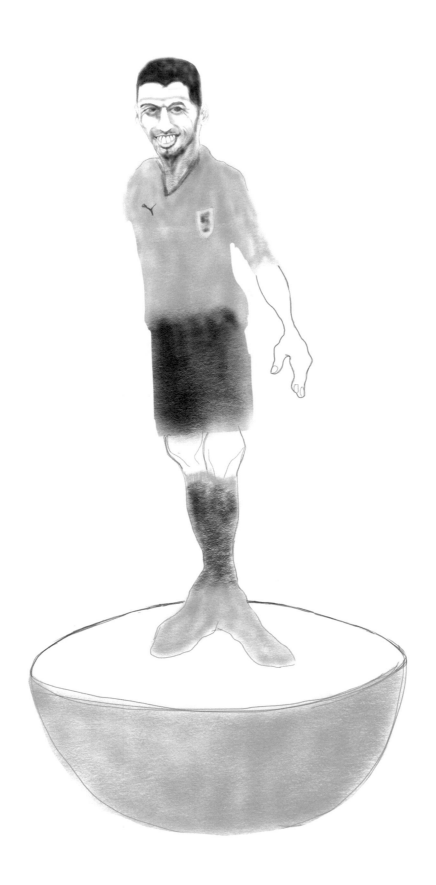

The Group of Six

Match 13.   Netherlands 2–1 Mexico (I break Mexican hearts with a late double)

Well, well, well … my tournament has finally kicked off big style, and my role in our team's success has been widely applauded by all the pundits who matter.

For those of you who have been asleep for the last twenty-four hours, we pulled off a staggering late comeback to beat Mexico 2–1 in Fortaleza and make the quarter-finals of the World Cup. A stunning goal from Giovani dos Santos and a string of magical saves from Guillermo Ochoa got Mexico to within two minutes of a spot in the last eight. But Louis van Gaal's decision to replace Robin van Persie with me paid off, as I was at the heart of the astonishing late comeback as we pulled off an unforgettable victory.

I nodded down from a corner for Wesley Sneijder with just two minutes left, and the Galatasaray playmaker drilled a stunning low shot into the bottom left corner. Extra time seemed our reward, but the game took another twist as Arjen Robben won a penalty almost three minutes into the six minutes of added time.

And it was yours truly who stepped up to the penalty spot. I had to wait a long time but kept my nerve to hammer my penalty low into the right-hand corner, sending the ever-impressive Ochoa the wrong way.

The only downside to our team's result was when one of the stray dogs who inhabit the streets next to the hotel jumped up onto the table on which the match was being contested, locked its teeth into the green baize of the pitch, pulled it sharply, and ran off with it back to the nearby favela, scattering the players, goalposts, floodlights, and stands all over the poolside patio.

Unfortunately, Ochoa was snapped in half at his knees in the melee, so he is unlikely to ever play again, given that Subbuteo's rules state only intact players are allowed to play in international matches. Small plastic hemispheres with no players, players snapped off at the knees, players with no heads—none of these are permitted in the Subbuteo World Cup.

But that was a minor irritation in the scheme of things. We had won our match, and I was clearly at the heart of our victory. Subbuteo it might have been, but World Cup football victories don't get much better than that.

Match 14.   Brazil 15–0 Little Chalfont (How to be promoted from mover to milk-shaker)

Down on the beaches of Rio and deep in the jungle of Manaus, something radical has been brewing. This isn't just football; it's not even a variant of futsal, but a radical departure from what we would traditionally describe as football or soccer.

What I'm bringing to the world's sports audiences now is a brand-new type of game. It's called RogerBall and combines the speed of soccer, the animalism of rugby, the intelligence of chess, the bonhomie of darts, and the simplicity of rock-paper-scissors. It's played by any number of people on any stage possible, played over any length of time; the first to 100 Rogers is proclaimed the winner.

I see the game being administered at the village, town, district, state, or national level. I see an international federation of RogerBall leagues in the not-too-distant future with yours truly as its democratically elected president, visiting every corner of our globe to proclaim the benefits of adopting this universally playable sport.

RogerBall is set to become an Olympic sport within the next ten years, with yours truly as its first international expert.

In the meantime, I look longingly at the torn green baize, the broken floodlights, and the despairing players and spectators who are strewn across the floor in various states of disrepair. Their little faces are frozen in shock, ecstasy, or astonishment. It is as if Mount Vesuvius surfaced here, in the heart of the Brazilian World Cup, just when we were least expecting it.

That flea-infested mongrel has caused chaos in the soccer world: Luis has gone AWOL in the favelas. The England, Spain, and Italy teams have all been packed away in their boxes sans heads, sans legs, sans teeth, sans eyes, sans taste, sans everything, as Mr Shakespeare threatened us on one of those wet Wednesday afternoons when we'd lost 73–nil to the juniors of Mrs Myrtle's class.

FIFA officials are currently in various states of hysteria and threatening to ground everyone, but I shall remain calm, bide my time, deflect the despair, and prepare myself the only way I know how: by continuing to sit on the substitute bench, sipping my 5,000-calorie milkshake, and plotting the next move for world domination.

We're now in a new generation of football makers and shakers. The RogerBall Universe is the only place to be right now.

If I make it back onto the pitch anytime soon, it will be a miracle.

Match 15.   Argentina 3–1 Germany (Matching heads, feet, and bumpsy daisy)

For all intents, purposes, and appearances, I am an aspiring, perspiring football player who has struggled to make a name for himself in the lower leagues since the first moment he tentatively put on a football boot. I have shuffled around football pitches huge and tiny, waterlogged and snowbound, dried up and toasted, knee-deep in manure, landmines, and other flotsam and jetsam of everyday life.

I may appear fat, slow, and balding with two left feet and no ball-to-foot coordination, but I am enthusiastic. And this quality of boundless enthusiasm is what marked me to my teachers as potential pitch fodder when it came to populating school football teams. It didn't matter that I couldn't play, it didn't matter that I couldn't count, and it didn't matter that I couldn't see; none of these things matter at school. What matters is that you are an enthusiast—always present, always keen, always ready, and always up for the kill.

So, whilst there are matches still to play, there is still time for the enthusiast to call in the jeweller from Bogotá, Terry Venables from French Guiana, and the Sisters of Mercy from Mexico. Between us, we'll provide the adhesives, paint, and fiddly fingers which will put our teams back together. We may have a motley collection of hemispherical stands, heads, torsos, and broken-off limbs scattered across the hotel patio, but before too long, our teams will be reassembled, albeit with a degree of artistic licence.

Bobby Charlton's head is attached to Maradona's torso, which in turn is firmly glued to the base of a Republic of Ireland player. Ronaldo's greaseproof head finds itself without a corpse and planted on the end of the wire hook that manoeuvres the goalkeeper across and out of the goal.

Before long, our zealousness gets the better of us all, and we start painting our own faces onto the recombinant little players, who look like they're warming up for their next match but with the same combination of shock, ecstasy, astonishment, and enthusiasm etched across their tiny, furrowed foreheads.

I may appear fat, slow, and balding with two left feet and no ball-to-foot coordination, but I am enthusiastic, and I have been called up for my team. And enthusiasm to the football gorilla is what petrol is to the fanatic.

The quarter-finals beckon, and I shall spare no quarter in demonstrating my enthusiasm for our beautiful game and its beautiful players, irrespective of how they're configured and whether their heads match their feet.

The Group of Six Results

Match 13.   Netherlands 2–1 Mexico
Match 14.   Brazil 15–0 Little Chalfont
Match 15.   Argentina 3–1 Germany

stuck out my right foot
PNG031 pretty g

The Quarter-Finals

Match 16.   Argentina–France: Match abandoned
(Shooing the shih-tzu off your shoes)

It's all very well, these WAGs and their interstellar boyfriends poncing around the beaches whilst all around them, football players are snapped in half at the waist, their cities burn, and the favelas crumble. But you know things have gone just a bit too far when you find yourself having to shoo a shih-tzu shit off your shoe because some mega-rich toy boy from FIFA has decided his dog needs to crap on the pavement and he's left the compound without the obligatory pooper-scooper, meaning us footballers in waiting have to deal with a shed load of shit on our kit just minutes before one of the most important matches of our lives.

That's right: I have finally been picked to start on the first team against France, in the first of the 2014 World Cup quarter-finals in Brazil. My teammates are focused, taciturn, and utterly dedicated to the task at hand: preparing for victory in a penalty shootout after 120 minutes. I, on the other hand, am focused, taciturn, and utterly dedicated to the task of shooing the FIFA shih-tzu shit off my training shoe. If there was ever a wrong time to be thinking about the contents of a shih-tzu's stomach, it's now, just hours before the biggest game of my life. What to use? Spit and polish? Acid? Shiatsu pressure around the FIFA official's throat?

I'm livid, and the team sense it and back off as if I am suddenly the source of the most odious-smelling vapours imaginable. Which I probably am. Even Luis, recently rehabilitated into the land of the living from his life of purgatory in a two-star hotel in downtown Ilhéus, is urging me to calm down, as I'm scaring him with my accusations, curses, and threats of revenge on all things shih-tzu.

That mangy mutt nearly wrecked our pitch, our lighting stands, and our teams; it nigh on destroyed our tournament, but there is no way on this earth that I am letting it ruin my place in history. I shall take the necessary steps after I have rehabilitated my trainers.

Me. You. FIFA man. Careful where you take that dog in future. First things first: baby wipes.

The Quarter-Finals Results

Match 16.   Argentina–France: Match abandoned

All quarter-finals were abandoned due to all teams' being in an inappropriate state of dress. Teams to progress to the semi-finals were drawn by lots. The matches will take place when the pitch and players can be fully repaired.

In the first semi-final, Germany will play Brazil; and in the second, the Netherlands will take on Argentina.

Whilst fans of the mighty Little Chalfont team might be disappointed to note that their team seems to have failed to qualify from the group of sixteen, we have been assured that they are planning an astonishing comeback, as soon as their players can be glued back together again.

The Semi-Finals

Match 17.   Brazil 7–1 Germany ('Nuff said)

Germany suffered the worst defeat in their footballing history as they were crushed 7–1 by Brazil in the World Cup semi-final in Belo Horizonte, and I had a modest but significant part to play in their downfall.

As well as being Germany's heaviest-ever defeat, it was also the biggest-ever victory in a World Cup semi-final, and the match which recorded the highest number of own goals ever.

The away side started brightly, but the Brazilian outfit took the lead after just eleven minutes as Thomas Müller side-footed home a diabolical own goal. And barely ten minutes later, Germany's World Cup dream imploded in horrifying style as the Brazilians scored three times in 179 seconds, with Klose, Kroos (2), and Khedira all taking leave of their collective senses by putting four (yes, four) goals in the wrong net, sometimes in spectacular style. This made the score 5–0 just before the half-hour mark, giving Brazil five goals in an eighteen-minute spell.

After the break, Germany came out looking determined and, for once, facing the right direction. They forced two outstanding saves from the Brazilian goalkeeper, Julio Cesar, but the home team soon regained control, and I was brought on late in the day to score twice with two superb (if I do say so myself) half volleys from the centre circle to make it 7–0.

In the dying moments, Mesut Ozil darted up the other end, where he scored the consolation goal.

Brazil are now the red-hot favourite to win their first World Cup at home, and I am carving out a place for myself in a side which has caused ripples of shock across the world.

As for Germany, wholesale changes are expected, as the nation suffered its largest and most humiliating defeat ever. We expect a run on the Euro and the possibility of rioting in Dresden, Passau, and Aachen. One thing we do know is that we are all aching with the seismic shifts that the global footballing community felt late into the night. Whether the European Union can withstand this level of cultural devastation is another matter.

I shall continue to practice, practice, practice for my apotheosis.

Match 18.   Brazil 1–7 Germany (The rules, *Les Mis*, and *Das Kapital*)

Once upon a time, whilst whiling away my time on the touch line at an away game in Lithuania, I wrote a play called *Rules of the Game*. It was premised on the notion that in the future, football would only be played in front of no more than ten people to prevent public disorder, young people would only be able to attend if accompanied by a grandparent, and street football would be forbidden.

The team's coach thought the major problem with the script was it required the reader to believe at least ten improbable things before breakfast, which made it hard to gauge the story's dramatic effectiveness. One of those things was the improbable proposition that somehow, on a World Cup stage, Germany would be humiliated one goal to seven by Brazil.

Improbable it may have been, but the play went through several rewrites, was produced in a small off-off-Broadway theatre, and soon hit commercial and artistic heights, touring the world as a multimillion-dollar blockbuster. You would now recognise it as *Les Mis*, but you probably don't know that it started life as a show about football hooliganism in the Balkans.

Now that we're in the quarter-finals, I'm reminded of the journey of that script and how, inadvertently, it made me an absolute fortune, so much that I can afford to spend the rest of my days toiling away on muddy football pitches, waiting for the big call: the chance to play in a World Cup final.

With potentially only two matches still to play, that call is tantalisingly close, as long as my team compadres don't throw away the moment in a fit of temperamental pique. There would be nothing worse than to get so close to a final only for it to disappear due to others' ineptitude and lack of commitment to the cause. But I have faith in them all, and they have faith in me.

Match 19.   Argentina 0–0 Netherlands (We can be heroes for a while)

Amazingly, and against intense local hostility, we edged out the Netherlands last night in a nervy penalty shootout (4–2) to set up a World Cup final with Germany after what was, let's face it, a dire goalless draw.

The liberated salamanders tried their best to liven up the proceedings by wandering over the pitch whenever the fancy took them, meaning that both sides showed little ambition to commit players forward in a cagy encounter. Neither me nor my Dutch counterpart was forced to make a meaningful save in normal time. In fact, I spent most of the game placing the salamanders back in their tank, it was that dull. But they were irrepressible in their desire to explore the freedom their newfound legs gave them, and they continued to disrupt both teams' efforts all afternoon.

After about three hours of fending off the salamanders, we opted to go into extra time as my pals Rodrigo and Maxi forced Jasper Cillessen into routine stops. But soon, the inevitable moment drew nigh, and penalties were in the offing.

It surprised everyone when I was sprung into the role of substitute goalkeeper. They had told me, "You gotta take one for team," in training that morning. So I did just that, and everyone was amazed when the manager swapped me in for his first-choice goalie just minutes before full time was up. This clearly unnerved the Dutch, but we held our nerve from the spot, scoring all four of our penalties whilst I made jaw-dropping, essential saves from Vlaar and Sneijder.

I was held aloft by my team, the other team, wives, girlfriends, swimming coaches, hot dog sellers, and even Luis Suarez, who recognised that his sulking was winning him no friends and certainly not the biggest prize of all, the World Cup itself.

My biggest moment, however—the final—awaits me on Sunday.

The Semi-Finals Results

Match 17.   **Brazil 7–1 Germany**
Match 18.   **Brazil 1–7 Germany**
Match 19.   **Argentina 0–0 Netherlands**

The Final

Match 20.   Germany 1–0 Argentina (No *me* in *team*? On the contrary ...)

After a month of trials, tribulations, hopes, fears, and guesswork, here it is, finally—my pièce de résistance.

It was a dull state of affairs until I struck a wonderful extra-time winner to beat Argentina 1–0 and claim the 2014 World Cup at the Estadio Maracana. I came off the bench to coolly chest and volley home a sublime goal after great work by me on the left to end a twenty-four-year wait for Die Mannschaft. It came with just seven minutes of extra time remaining, and saw my team secure a fourth world title and become the first European team to win the tournament in South America.

The match was marginally interesting at the beginning when it became clear that I had sustained an injury in pre-match training, but I was then substituted by me with me at short notice. The game faded badly in the second period and looked all set for a shootout until I struck.

My Argentinian me blazed a glorious opportunity wide early on in extra time, and I had my moment of redemption stolen away shortly afterwards when I was flagged offside while finishing off a sublime move involving me and me. My super-sub effort was beaten away by me before I somehow contrived to crash a free header against the post from inside the six-yard box at the stroke of halftime. I commiserated with myself and myself, but it was a tough moment to swallow.

As Lionel Messi, I could and should have made it my World Cup moment after the restart, but I dragged the ball wide, and that proved to be the best of the action until extra time, when I tested me, but immediately tested myself by lobbing the ball off target. My teammates congratulated me for the attempted shot, and my other teammates for the superlative save. I finally broke through with my wonderful finish, and Argentina couldn't recover as my side held firm to move level with Italy on four world titles—just one behind Brazil, of all teams.

It has been a roller-coaster of a ride, and one that me and my teammates of me, me, me, and me will never forget for the rest of our lives. In the meantime, it's back to the day job of the lower divisions and away fixtures in Little Chalfont. This football gorilla has finally made his mark.

The Final Results

Match 20.   **Germany 1–0 Argentina**

About the Author

Nick Owen was awarded an MBE for services to arts-based businesses in 2012 and is passionate about generating culturally inspiring and socially engaging creative practice within educational contexts both nationally and internationally.

He has worked in the creative and cultural industries across the public, private and social enterprise sectors in the East Midlands, Merseyside and Cumbria whilst committed to developing international links with partners in Bulgaria, Chile, India and Serbia amongst others. Visiting Professor at the School of Human and Health Sciences at the University of Huddersfield, he is also a keen cyclist, tennis player, fiction writer and Vinyl DJ.

Recent publications include:

Confessions of an Ageing Tennis Player, 2021, Nick Owen Publishing Ltd, Lincoln

Owen, N., Clark, L. and Farley, C. (2021) Expressive Arts and Design in The Early Years Foundation Stage: Theory and Practice (4th Edition, ed. Palaiologou, I.) London: SAGE.

No Such Thing as an Englishman: poems from an Irritated England, 2020, Amazon

Russell, L. and Owen, N. (2013) The Creative Research Process: Delights and Difficulties. LEARNing Landscapes, Autumn 2012 Vol.6 No.1 - Creativity: Insights, Directions and Possibilities. Québec: LEARN.

For further information please contact nick@nickowenpublishing.co.uk

Printed in the United States
by Baker & Taylor Publisher Services